Water Cycle

WATER FACT FILE

Water is amazing!

It is vital for all life on Earth.

It covers about 70% of Earth's surface.

It freezes solid at 0°C.

It boils at 100°C.

Written by Dr Malcolm Rose

Illustrated by Sean Sims

EGMONT
We bring stories to life

Book Band: White

Adapted from *The Adventures of Water* first published in Great Britain 2015

Water Cycle first published in Great Britain 2017
by Red Shed, an imprint of Egmont UK Limited
The Yellow Building, 1 Nicholas Road, London W11 4AN

www.egmont.co.uk

Consultancy by Dr Patricia Macnair and Ryan Marek

ISBN 978 1 4052 8493 6

A CIP catalogue record for this book is available from The British Library.

Printed in Singapore
65792/1

Series and book banding consultant: Nikki Gamble

Water Cycle

Reading Ladder

Contents

Introduction

Water has been around for millions and millions of years. There is an awful lot of it on Earth – about 1,369 million cubic kilometres, which is enough to fill 550 million million Olympic-size swimming pools! And it gets almost everywhere.

All about water

Most of our water is older than the planets. It was in the dust and gas clouds that made Earth. It may also have arrived in icy comets and watery asteroids that bombarded Earth millions of years ago.

Dinosaurs may have splashed around in some of the water that comes out of your tap!

One molecule of water is made up of one oxygen atom with two hydrogen atoms attached to it. Water's chemical formula is H_2O.

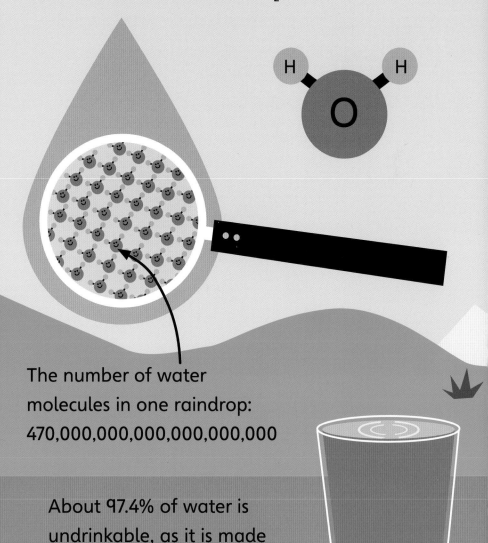

The number of water molecules in one raindrop: 470,000,000,000,000,000,000,000

About 97.4% of water is undrinkable, as it is made up of the oceans, seas and salty groundwater.

What is water?

A lot of the time, water is a liquid. But sometimes it is a solid. And sometimes it will be blown around by the wind as a gas (water vapour).

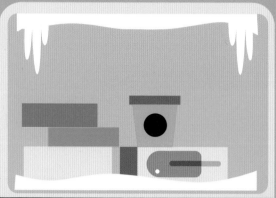

When the temperature rises to above 0°C, frozen water turns to liquid.

Water can be frozen solid as ice, snow, frost or hail. Water freezes solid at 0°C.

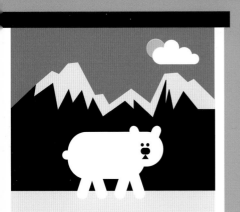

Water carves up the surface of our planet. Rivers and glaciers hollow out valleys, and seawater shapes the coastline.

If you heat water until it boils, it becomes a gas and blows away into the atmosphere.

Less than 1% is available as drinking water.

Taking a drink

Water goes into your body in the form of food and drink. All drinks contain water, and even solid-looking food has some water.

Water and food go into your mouth. Then down your throat and gullet and into your stomach.

About 60% of an adult human body is made of water.

A human baby can be up to 75% water.

A jellyfish is 95% water.

A human can survive without food for about two months, but less than one week without drinking water.

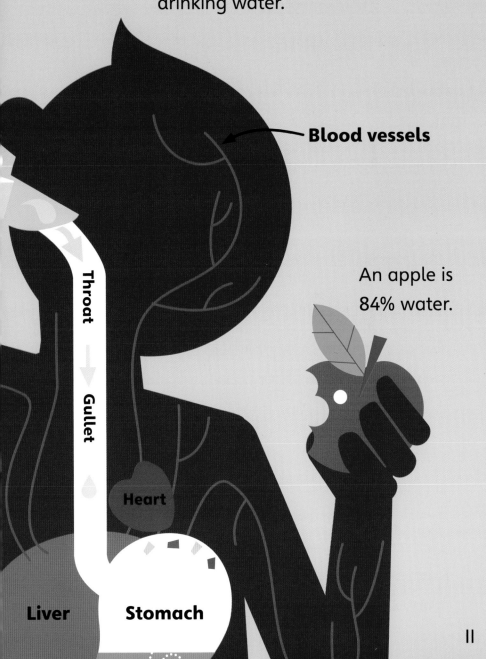

Blood vessels

An apple is 84% water.

Throat

Gullet

Heart

Liver   **Stomach**

Body journey

Food and drink are broken down in your stomach before continuing on their way. Nutrients are sent off into your bloodstream to give you energy. Waste is passed out in wee and poo.

Liver

Kidney

Food is broken down by acid and proteins into a watery mush, which is squirted into your intestines.

In the intestines, most of the water and nutrients pass into the bloodstream. The remaining solid waste and some water is stored in the rectum until you do a poo.

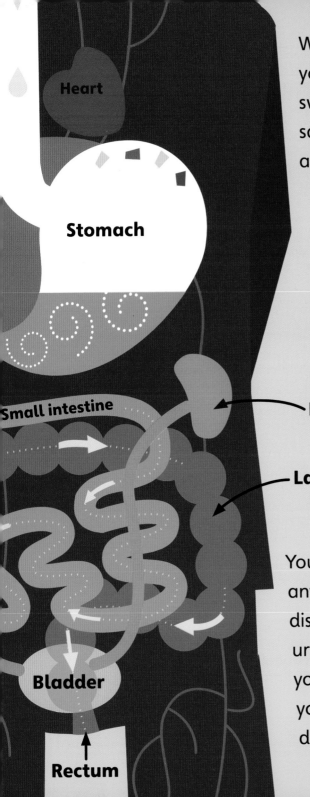

Heart

Stomach

Water also leaves your body via sweat, blood, saliva, snot, tears and breathing.

Small intestine

Kidney

Large intestine

Bladder

Rectum

Your bladder holds any water and dissolved wastes as urine (wee). When your bladder is full, you get the urge to dash to the toilet.

13

Water treatment

Where does the watery waste (sewage) goes after you flush the toilet? It goes to a water treatment plant, where it is cleaned. Some becomes drinking water!

Rainwater pipe

1. Toilet paper, rags, bottles, branches, stones and other rubbish are filtered out using a screen.

Sewage pipe

Waste water pipe

2. Smaller stones, grit, sand and broken glass settle onto the bottom.

3. In a special tank, more solid stuff – such as human poo – sinks to the bottom as sludge.

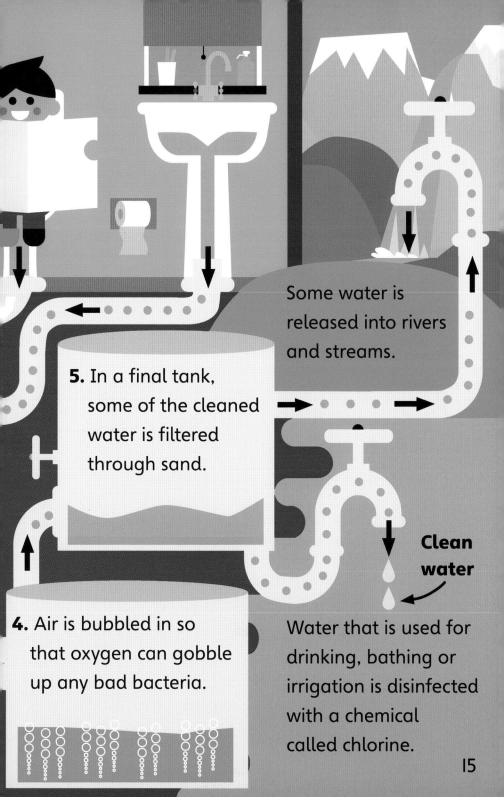

Some water is released into rivers and streams.

5. In a final tank, some of the cleaned water is filtered through sand.

4. Air is bubbled in so that oxygen can gobble up any bad bacteria.

Clean water

Water that is used for drinking, bathing or irrigation is disinfected with a chemical called chlorine.

15

Round and round

Water travels round and round in a journey called the water cycle. There is only a certain amount of water on Earth and it is important that it is recycled.

CONDENSATION

1. Water vapour in the air comes from the sea (evaporation) or from plants (transpiration) and forms clouds (condensation).

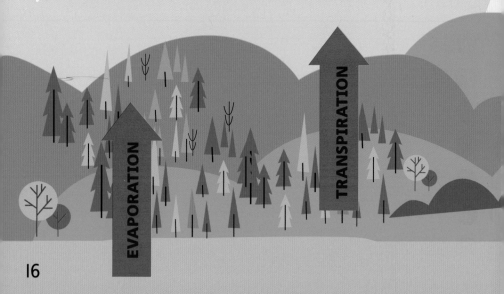

EVAPORATION

TRANSPIRATION

2. Water vapour in the clouds turns into watery drops that fall to the ground as rain, snow or hail (precipitation).

PRECIPITATION

3. Precipitation eventually runs back into the sea (runoff) and the whole cycle begins again when the seawater is heated by the sun (evaporation).

RUN OFF

Rain

If droplets in a cloud combine, or if more water condenses onto them, they get bigger. They fall to earth as rain when they become too heavy to float in the sky.

Rainclouds look dark from underneath. This is because less sunlight can get through thicker clouds containing lots of water.

Around 45,000 thunderstorms form around the world every day.

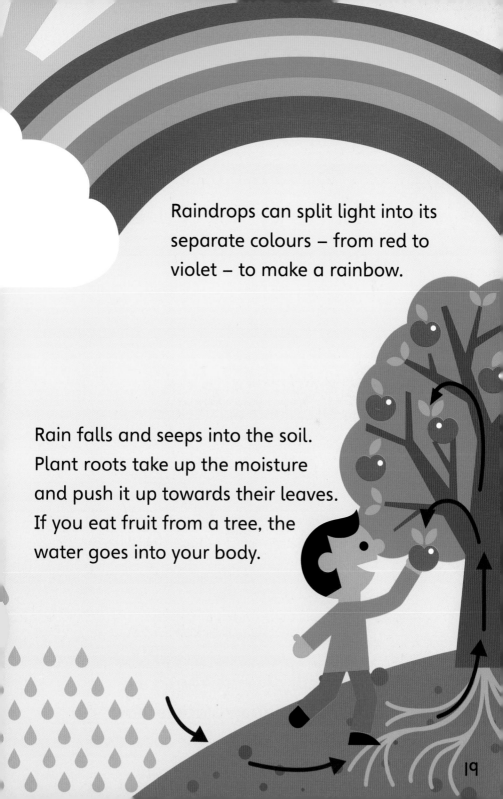

Raindrops can split light into its separate colours – from red to violet – to make a rainbow.

Rain falls and seeps into the soil. Plant roots take up the moisture and push it up towards their leaves. If you eat fruit from a tree, the water goes into your body.

Snow and ice

If the air is cold enough, water droplets
in a cloud will turn into ice crystals.
These can float down as snowflakes,
or pelt down as icy hail, or sleet
(a mixture of snow and rain).

Over hundreds of years, the snow
can become a glacier. Glaciers move
slowly downhill towards the sea.

All snowflakes have six points. This is due to the way that water molecules line up when they freeze.

Some water falls as snow onto frozen land high in the mountains or near the North or South poles.

Snowflakes can take more than 45 minutes to reach the ground.

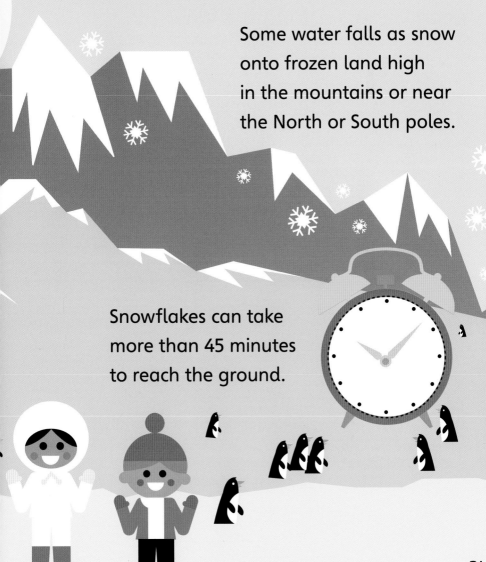

River power

Scrubbed nice and clean, most of the water released into a river heads to the sea. But all sorts of adventures can happen along the way.

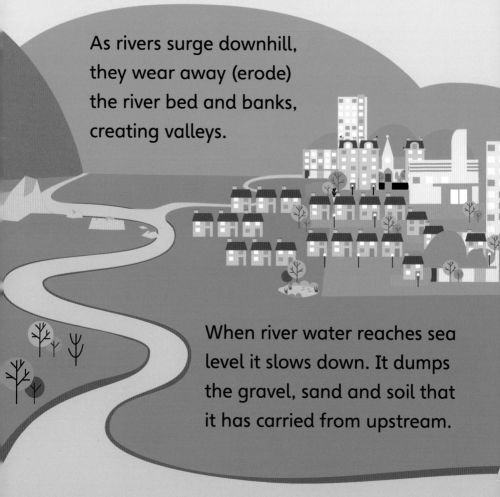

As rivers surge downhill, they wear away (erode) the river bed and banks, creating valleys.

When river water reaches sea level it slows down. It dumps the gravel, sand and soil that it has carried from upstream.

Water running downhill hits the blades of a water wheel (turbine) and makes them turn. This movement is converted into electricity.

Rivers are useful for transporting goods by boat. This is why so many towns and cities are built beside rivers.

Rivers are also great for windsurfing, water skiing, fishing and swimming.

All at sea

Water swirls round the planet in seas and oceans. It is warmed by the sun, whipped up by the wind, and churned by the waves. The water at the surface evaporates over millions of years, leaving salt behind.

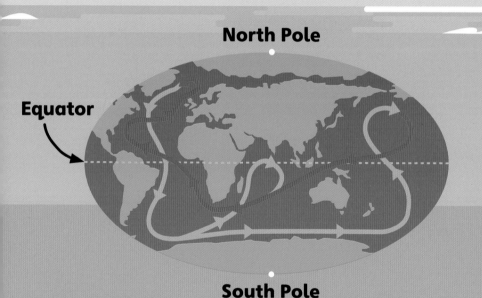

Warm water (red) from near the Equator flows towards the poles. Cold water (blue) flows back from the poles towards the Equator.

The sea supports up to 80% of all living species on Earth.

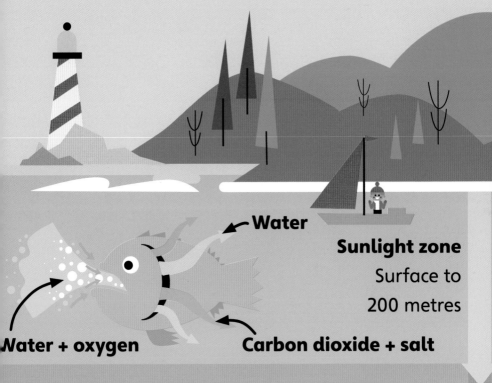

Water

Sunlight zone
Surface to
200 metres

Water + oxygen

Carbon dioxide + salt

A fish breathes by sucking in water. Oxygen dissolved in the water trickles into its blood vessels. Water forced out of its gills carries away carbon dioxide and salt.

Twilight zone
200 metres to
1,000 metres

Deepest oceans

Some water in the deepest parts of the oceans is below 0°C. It remains liquid because the salt stops it turning to ice.

Sometimes water heated by volcanic activity to more than 350°C gushes out through a hole in the sea floor. These holes are called black smokers or hydrothermal vents.

More human beings have walked on the Moon than have travelled to the deepest parts of the oceans.

Angler fish live in total darkness so they make their own light from chemicals in their bodies.

Midnight zone
1,000 metres and deeper

It is completely dark here.

27

People and water

Clean water is needed in houses, schools, factories, restaurants, hospitals, laundries, car washes, hotels and lots of other places. Think of all the toilets that have to be flushed!

A huge amount of water is needed for farming. It is used to keep animals alive, irrigate crops and spread fertilizers.

Water in rivers and lakes can be used to fight forest fires. A helicopter can scoop up a huge amount of water to throw over the flames.

Glossary

acid   A chemical in the stomach that breaks down food and destroys any harmful bacteria.

atom   The smallest particle of a substance that can exist by itself

bacteria   One-celled organisms that can only be seen with a microscope. Some bacteria are good and some harmful.

chemicals   Substances such as water, salt and gold; everything is made of chemicals, including you.

condensation   When water vapour cools and forms droplets. These may form clouds.

evaporation   When a liquid escapes into the air as a gas.

freeze   When a liquid is cooled so much that it becomes solid, for example water turning into ice.

☀ Fun facts

The world's tallest water slide is Verrückt in Kansas City, USA. It has a drop of over 50 metres.

glacier   A huge mass of ice that flows like a very slow river over land.

hydrogen   A colourless gas that is the lightest in the universe.

irrigate   To supply with water, usually to water crops.

molecule   Two or more atoms linked together to make the smallest part of a chemical substance.

nutrient   A substance that is needed for growth and a healthy life.

precipitation   Water falling from the sky as rain, snow, hail or sleet.

transpiration   The passage of water vapour from plant leaves into the atmosphere.

vapour   Particles of moisture in the air that can be seen, for example as clouds or smoke.

The wettest places on Earth are Mawsynram, India and Tutendo, Colombia. Both have about 12 metres of rain each year.

Index